To Joanna, my dino–buddy—S. C.

To Alvise and Sofia—A. F.

Text copyright © 2017 by Stephanie Calmenson

Illustrations copyright © 2017 by AntonGionata Ferrari

All Rights Reserved

HOLIDAY HOUSE is registered in the U.S. Patent and Trademark Office.

Printed and bound in April 2017 at Tien Wah Press, Johor Bahru, Johor, Malaysia.

The artwork was created with watercolors, acrylics, india ink, collage, and digital tools.

www.holidayhouse.com

First Edition

1 3 5 7 9 10 8 6 4 2

Library of Congress Cataloging-in-Publication Data is available.

ISBN 9780823436729 (hardcover)

NO HONKING ALLOWED!

BY
STEPHANIE
CALMENSON

ILLUSTRATED BY
ANTONGIONATA
FERRARI

Holiday House  New York

Come for a ride in my dino-car.
I like to go fast! I like to go far!

We'll buckle our seat belts.
That's for safety, you know.
Click! We're all set.
Now we can go.

I love the sounds
my new car makes.

goes the engine!

SCREEEECHHHHH

go the brakes!

Slow down, Rex!

HONK! That's my horn.
It's loud as can be.
HONK! HONK! HONK!
It's perfect for me!

Look at that driver
speeding to town.
Can I honk to remind her
she'd better slow down?

Surprise! Surprise!
I see someone I know.
I'll honk my horn
and wave hello!

No honking allowed!
There's another sign.

That dog walker's leash
is all twisted up.
I'll honk so he'll know
to untangle his pup.

See that cute buggy
with kids passing by?
I'll make them happy
when I honk to say hi.

Don't honk.
You'll scare them.

That boom box blasting
makes me frown.
I'll honk and holler,
"Turn it down!"

No honking. No hollering.

A dino's littering.
That's really bad.
I'll honk and tell him
it makes me mad.

Listen! Sirens!
Woo-woo-woo!
A fire truck's coming.
It's got to get through!

Nobody's moving.
The streets are a mess!
I've got to honk now.
Stego, please tell me yes!

One honk didn't help,
and the truck's getting near.
I must honk again,
long, loud and clear.

Go for it, Rex!

Sorry.
No honking allowed!

The fire truck made it.
I helped clear the way.
Can I honk for happy?
What do you say?

Rex, honking's for safety.
That is the rule.
For anything else, it just isn't cool.

We had fun, dino-buddy.

You helped the fire truck go.

Will you help me pay the ticket?

Huh?

Pleeease?

Well, okay.